Toad Getting Married

Written by Ken Metcalfe

With illustrations by Neil Chapman

Ken Metcalfe was born in Lancashire and worked in the Engineering Industry until he retired in 2001. He now lives in North Cornwall with his wife, Val. He has four children and twelve grandchildren. When he's not writing stories about Toad, he likes gardening, walking and an occasional game of golf.

First published 2016 by Mereo Books

ISBN: 978-1-86151-463-9

This is Toad. His real name is Syd Toad, but he *hates* his first name and never, ever uses it. So everyone in the part of Africa where he lives just calls him Toad.

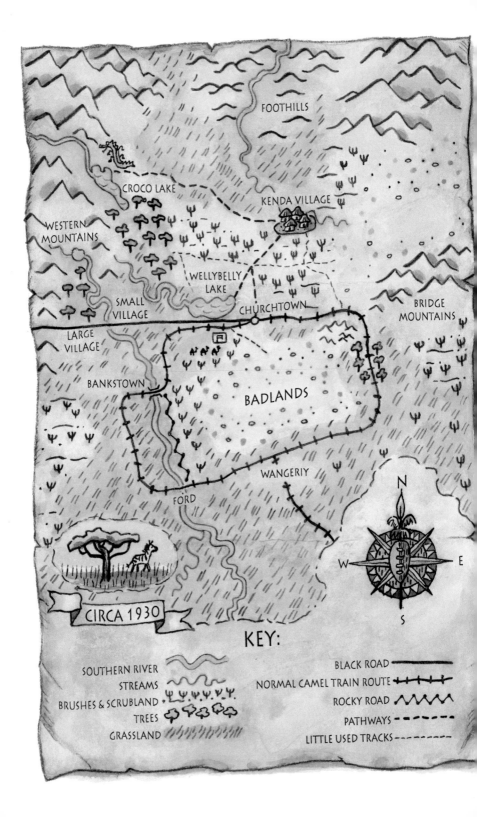

Contents

Chapter One

Wednesday

The peaks of the Western Mountains were lit up as lightning streaked across the horizon. Thunder crashed and banged and could be heard up to 50 miles away, whilst the skies above the mountains were full of dark clouds that seemed to be swirling about, round and round the peaks. Torrential rain fell for hours and hours and hours and flowed into the dry riverbeds, rapidly filling them up.

Toad looked over to the mountains and was rather concerned. He liked wet weather, and although normally there wasn't that much rain where he lived, the lake certainly needed a top-up and would get one when the streams filled up and flowed down to Wellybelly. It was the volume of rain that worried Toad. If there was too much, it could create a lot of damage and destroy the very dry landscape, uprooting shrubs and trees and washing everything away.

Toad was growing tired, as the air was heavy, so as usual when he couldn't do anything about a problem, he went to sleep under his favourite stone by the edge of the lake. He began to dream. It was Wednesday and he was dreaming of Saturday when he was to be married. Actually all the toads in the Wellybelly area were to be married that Saturday. It was the annual toad marriage ceremony, and boy was Toad going to enjoy himself! He had no idea whom he was going to marry, but there were so many lady toads available that he was confident of getting himself a big, fat cuddly one.

Just as his dream was getting interesting, Toad was rudely awakened. He appeared to be flying through the air and, an instant later, he came to earth with a bump and landed on something very hard, whilst a multitude of small, medium and large stones rained down upon him.

Toad slipped in and out of consciousness. Time passed. How much time Toad didn't know, but as he regained his senses, somewhere in the background he could hear voices. Human voices. All Toad knew about humans was that they were stupid, so he knew he wouldn't get any help from them.

The atmosphere had changed, and there was a fresher feel to the weather. He couldn't hear the thunder, and the mountains seemed farther away. He listened intently to the conversation between the two humans.

"I got you these stones that you asked for," said a deep male voice. "I collected lots of them from Wellybelly Lake, just like you wanted." A door slammed and the crunch of footsteps reverberated through the truck's metal sides. "See here in the back, I've got you a little bonus - just look at this lovely fat toad," said the man. "It'll keep all the flies and midges away from your lake."

A moment later Toad seemed to be flying again. He landed with a splash in some water, but a lake it was not. More like a muddy little pond.

"Ignorant human!" Toad shouted. "You are a stupid man! I am not fat! Only lady toads are fat! And how dare you remove me from Wellybelly when I am about to be married and then throw me here and there!" Then Toad screamed even louder, "TAKE ME BACK AT ONCE!"

"Croak, croak" chuckled the lady, "croak, croak. Oh, how sweet! Tommy – isn't he sweet?"

Toad had met all the animals around the Wellybelly area, and with the exception of humans and snakes, he could converse with all of them. That was because he was a 'Speakabody' who could communicate with lots of other creatures. "Ugh, snakes!" he said out loud, and shivered at the thought of them. Humans - well they were certainly not as scary as snakes. However, when he spoke to them, all they ever said to him was "croak, croak." He hadn't a clue what "croak, croak" meant, but it confirmed to Toad that all humans were stupid. They could also be dangerous, cruel and insensitive, which had been confirmed once again by Tommy throwing him all over the place.

Toad knew he had to escape. Yes, the pond might provide him with some food for a day or two, but he had to get back to Wellybelly Lake for his wedding. He didn't want to let anyone down and he was absolutely sure that if he didn't turn up for the wedding celebrations, he would be missed.

From just under the surface of the pond he listened carefully, trying to discover just where he was, what day it was and how much time he had to get back to Wellybelly for the marriage celebrations. Tommy was still talking to the woman, but in the background he heard another noise - a camel. Toad knew that camels travelled past the Wellybelly area regularly in both directions. They were used to deliver large loads into the outlying districts. Perhaps the camel could help him. Toad decided it would be safer to wait until dusk and then try to find the camel.

* * *

"Hello there," called Toad as the sun began setting in the sky. Toad knew he would have to wait a while for the camel to answer. It wasn't being rude. It just always seemed to take camels a really long time to answer and they didn't always understand the words they were asked. In Toad's opinion camels were also stupid, but they weren't as stupid as humans.

"Hello," came the reply at last. "My eyesight is poor and I cannot see you very well in this light. May I know who you are?"

"My name is Toad and I'm from Wellybelly Lake," answered Toad. "Please may I know your name too?"

Another very long pause. Then the camel said, "I am known as Old Camel. What are you doing all this way from Wellybelly?"

"I was brought here by some careless humans," explained Toad, "and I need to get back there in a hurry." There was a note of excitement in his voice as he realised Old Camel might be able to help him to do this. He decided to ask a few questions and see what happened next.

"What is the date?" said Toad. Saturday the 18th was the date of the marriage celebrations, and as he had no idea how long he had been unconscious or how far he had to travel, he didn't know whether he would miss all the partying. If that happened it would be a disaster, as Toad considered himself to be special, so his future wife would miss the experience of her life. Unfortunately, Toad's pomposity sometimes led him to imagine he would make a perfect husband for some lucky lady toad. This time it misled him into believing that he was the most desirable toad in Wellybelly Lake.

Old Camel thought for a while. His reply took even longer than Toad had expected, probably because he hadn't understood the question about the date. Eventually he answered, "A date is a delicious fruit which grows on trees. I think they are very tasty."

Here we go, thought Toad, *I'll have to ask this camel an easier question.*

"OK," he said hesitantly. "Do you know what day it is?"

Old Camel did not wish to be unhelpful, but he wasn't sure what the word 'day' meant either. He had heard the word Wezzday said by the master, or something that sounded like Wezzday, and that word had day in it, so he decided that's the answer he would give Toad. After what seemed an age, Old Camel replied that he thought it was Wezzday.

Wow, thought Toad, Old Camel must mean Wednesday. If it was really Wednesday, then he hadn't lost any days yet and he still had time to get back to Wellybelly to be married. He was still a little sceptical of anything old Camel said, so he decided to pursue his line of questioning.

Toad asked as gently and politely as he could, "When do you go to Wellybelly?"

Eventually Old Camel replied, "Thursty. I always go to Wellybelly when Thursty. Why do you want to know?"

Toad knew he had to be careful because it sounded as though Old Camel was going to Wellybelly tomorrow. However camels can be sensitive and, although the information he had received was good information, it was not necessarily correct. So Toad decided to be on his best behavior when seeking help from Old Camel.

"I was wondering if you could assist me," said Toad, carefully and politely. "I need to get back to Wellybelly for a meeting." It was no good telling Old Camel about his proposed wedding, as camels had no idea what marriage was.

"I suppose I could help," said Old Camel. "There are some parcels stacked up across the road and wrapped in cloth. If you climb into one of those sacks, the master will load them onto my back in the morning."

Toad was about to ask Old Camel where he was when he heard a strange noise. It was a sound he had not heard before, loud but quite pleasant. He asked what the noise was.

After a pause Old Camel replied, "They are church bells. The Churchtown bell ringers are practicing."

Wow! thought Toad. *Churchtown is the next town on the black road from Wellybelly.* He knew now that he wasn't that far away from home. Churchtown was where the new black road ended. If anyone wanted to travel farther east, they would have to use camels, or walk.

Toad was now feeling weary. The conversation with Old Camel had taken well over an hour and he couldn't cope with any more. So he said his thanks, wished him goodnight and made his way over to the sacks.

Chapter Two

Thursday

Surprisingly, Toad slept but he awoke with an unusual floating sensation. He was about to poke his head out of the sack when he remembered where he was. His night-time shelter was being lifted onto the back of a camel.

Toad waited patiently. When he realized that the journey to Wellybelly had begun, he decided to have a look round and see where he was. The camel seemed to roll from side to side as he ambled along, so Toad had to be careful in case he fell off.

"Hi" said Toad speaking to the back of the camel's head.

The reply took ages. "Who is that?" asked the camel, but this time he seemed to have a much deeper voice.

"It's me, Toad," said Toad. "You remember from last night? You said you would help me and take me to Wellybelly."

Eventually the camel said indignantly, "I most certainly did not say that!"

Toad thought for a while and looked ahead. There was one very dark brown camel in front, but he didn't look old. Toad didn't feel very safe on the back of his camel so carefully had a quick glance behind. There was one other camel following him that could be Old Camel whom he had spoken to last night, but as it had been getting dark he couldn't be sure. However he was on a camel, the middle of three camels in a camel train. Suddenly it dawned on him that his load had been put on a different camel. All three of them were carrying the same sacks.

There were hundreds of flies and midges following the camel train and buzzing around Toad's head. "Breakfast!" said Toad out loud and proceeded to feast on the bounty before him. "Maybe now I will be able to think clearly and work out what to do!"

He decided that somehow he would have to contact the other camel, his friend from yesterday called Old Camel, as the one he was travelling on seemed rather grumpy and he didn't fancy telling him the story of how he had to get to Wellybelly. That would take all day. There were levels of stupidity even within camels and Toad had decided that this camel was definitely the most stupid one he had met. However, Toad knew that he regularly made snap decisions and some of them could be wrong. This was soon confirmed. He was put in his place when the camel introduced himself as Gruff Camel and said, "If you want to go to Wellybelly, why have you chosen to go this way?"

Toad was caught off guard. He looked around and soon understood what the camel was saying about the direction they were going. The camel train was travelling in an easterly direction and Wellybelly was definitely west of where he had met Camel. The sun was in the north east, so Gruff Camel was correct. He was not as stupid as Toad thought.

Toad tried not to panic. He decided to think very carefully before he spoke to this creature again. He knew his very future depended on getting some help and, at this moment, Gruff Camel was his only hope. So he decided to try to get a conversation going with the animal. In his most pleasant voice he asked Gruff Camel a question, knowing that it would be some time before the answer came.

"Will you help me please?" said Toad beseechingly. "I need to get to Wellybelly by Saturday."

Toad decided to count how long it took for the camel to answer. He counted to thirty before he got a reply.

"Yes," said Gruff Camel.

Toad waited a bit longer. Knowing camels as he did, he knew "Yes" could be the full answer, or there could be a bit more answer to follow. Toad really couldn't decide whether this camel was more or less intelligent than Old Camel, but he soon found out. Gruff Camel had taken his time to answer because he had a lot to say. Eventually he began his reply. "We should pass another camel train sometime today," he said, "and it will be going in the opposite direction. If you can jump onto an overhanging tree branch you can wait there for the camel train to pass underneath and drop down onto one of the camels. You should then be travelling in the direction of Wellybelly."

Toad had never heard a camel say so much in one sentence.

Almost immediately he changed his opinion of the animal. *This is most certainly a fine camel*, thought Toad, *and as I really need his help, I must try to be as respectful as possible.* However Toad was finding it tiring acting out of character and he was also worn out with the amount of time it took him to get answers from the camel. So he crept wearily back into one of the sacks for a quick nap.

"Toad" he heard the camel call. Then "TOAD!" once again, only much louder. "There are some trees coming up."

"Yes, yes" said Toad impatiently, trying not to sound as if he had just woken up. He got out of the sack, crept up onto Gruff Camel's head and looked into the distance. Gruff Camel had a large tuft of hair on the top of his head and Toad clung onto this to prevent himself from falling off. He peeped through the gap in Gruff Camel's tufty hair and could see some mountains rising in front of him and a circular set of rocks on his right, but try as he could he couldn't see any trees. He knew that his eyesight was really good close to, but he still didn't think it was that bad at seeing into the distance, nor did he think that camels could see further than toads.

He was about to ask Gruff Camel where the trees were when, without warning, the dark brown camel who was leading turned sharply right down a track, heading in a southerly direction. As the others followed, the track sloped down slightly and in the distance Toad could see an avenue of trees. The trees were some distance away and they were a bright fresh green colour, flush with the first growth of spring.

"Wow!" exclaimed Toad. "Thank you so much for awakening me. Um, no sorry, alerting me that these trees were coming up. You really are being a true friend. Could you please tell me which will be the best tree to climb onto?"

Again there was the inevitable pause, but halfway towards the trees, Gruff Camel spoke. "Toad," he said, "please listen carefully, for what I am about to tell you to do will not be easy – well, not for a toad. However, it is you that wishes to go to Wellybelly."

Toad felt quite indignant that Gruff Camel should think he couldn't manage to get onto the trees, but he decided to be a little humble, knowing that he really needed the creature's help.

"I'm listening," said Toad seriously. "Please carry on."

They were almost at the trees when Gruff Camel spoke again.

"Toad," he said softly, "shortly we are going to stop under the shade of the trees for a few minutes. When we set off again I will select an appropriate tree and then try to lift my head up towards the branches to enable you to climb onto the tree. Try to be as quiet as possible because I don't want the man at the back to find out that I've helped you. The one who leads us is really kind and has always lived on this land. The one at the back is called Billy Johnson and he is the boss's son. He is horrible and cruel and will hit us with sticks for no reason."

Toad began to realize the enormity of the task ahead and also to appreciate just how much his new friend was doing for him.

The camel train arrived at the trees and stopped in the shade for a short while. The third camel, who was so thin and bony sat down to rest, much to the disappointment of Billy who grumbled at him. Toad realized this must be Old Camel he had spoken to last night, and felt sorry for him as Billy grumbled some more and gave him a prod with his crop. Toad knew that all humans were not the same. He had heard stories from other animals that some of the humans who were native to this land understood all the animals. Some of them could talk to them as well, but as Toad had never met one, he didn't believe these stories. He spoke to Gruff Camel, feeling rather guilty because he had thought so badly of him at first.

"One day, if you ever need my help," he said, "you must come and find me in Wellybelly Lake and I will repay my debt" he said. "Just tell me when and I will be ready."

Toad again waited for the reply, which took some considerable time.

"Thank you, Toad," said Gruff Camel. "That means a lot to me. Now it appears that we are ready to go, so I will take you to the best tree I can find."

The leading camel, who was called Brown Camel for obvious reasons started to walk away led by the local man. Gruff Camel followed, but broke away and gradually strayed towards a tree. Billy was still at the back, trying to get Old Camel up off the

ground, but he was having difficulty and getting increasingly cross. He shouted at Old Camel, "Get up, you lazy old bag of bones!" and raised his crop as if to beat him.

Just then, out of the corner of his eye, Billy noticed Gruff Camel. He appeared to be going sideways and reaching up towards a tree. Billy turned round and started to run towards him.

"Quickly, Toad, up you go before Billy comes," urged Gruff Camel. Toad mustered himself, shut his eyes and took a leap of faith. Miraculously he landed on a thin branch covered with lots of leaves. He clung on as if his life depended on it - which it did! Below him he heard a terrible crying sound. Billy had come up behind Gruff Camel and hit him with all his might with the riding crop he carried. "Get back into line!" he bellowed. Gruff Camel changed direction as quickly as he could and started to follow Brown Camel.

Toad climbed a little higher and peeped through the leaves to see what was going on. He saw the local man tie up Brown Camel and pull Gruff Camel in behind. Then he began to walk back towards Billy and Old Camel. Billy had returned to the poor creature and was also beating him with his crop to make him get up. The local man was smaller than Billy, but he spoke to him with authority and told Billy that his father would be very unhappy if the delivery did not arrive on time and even more unhappy if his camels were unable to work again. So, very politely, he asked Billy to go to the front of the camel train and said he would follow on a little bit later when he had given the old camel time to recover. Reluctantly Billy did as he was asked. He was cursing the camels and cursing the other man, but the mention of his father's name had made him see sense. Billy's father was very fond of his camels and not a man you wanted to upset.

* * *

"YUM, YUM!" When Toad heard that noise, it made him shiver with fear. He knew exactly what "YUM, YUM" meant. There was a snake nearby, perhaps even in this tree. Toad was in a precarious position, clinging onto the branch for dear life, with a big drop below him that would surely kill him if he fell. Yet somehow he had to cling on and escape from this horrible snake which had one thing in mind and that was to make Toad his next meal.

Toad knew the countdown to his imminent death all too well. Back at Wellybelly Lake there were quite a few snakes and Toad had seen some of his friends disappear into their mouths, never to return again. Snakes seemed to get more excited the closer they got to their prey, and began by saying "YUM, YUM." When they got closer they would say "YUM, YUM, YUM" and, just before they ate you, they would say, "YUM-YUM, YUM-YUM." Then they would open their jaws and swallow you whole. *Ugh!* thought Toad. *What a way to die!* Toad resolved that he would not die in such a disgusting way, becoming someone's lunch.

Then he heard rustling sounds above him and the ominous "YUM, YUM, YUM" came again. Toad knew he could not hide but, at the same time, he couldn't bring himself to jump off the tree to a certain death, so he backed away to the very edge of the branch hoping that the snake could not follow. Above him the head of a large green and yellow snake jabbed through the leaves. "YUM-YUM, YUM-YUM!" said the snake, opening his enormous mouth and showing Toad two very purple-looking fangs and a red flashing tongue.

"NO!" screamed Toad.

Meanwhile, below, Old Camel was struggling to get up after the beating he had taken, so the local man looked around for something he could use to help it. He found some leaves growing on a bush at the side of the track. He squashed them all together in a small bowl he carried until they became a gooey liquid. Then he picked up a flat stick and rubbed the squashy solution onto the knee joint of the old beast.

"This will help you, old friend" he said. "If you can stand up and begin walking slowly, you will notice the pain will get less the longer you walk. Before we reach Wangeriy, I will find some better treatment for you."

Old Camel struggled to his feet and started to walk slowly. "Thank you," he said. "I will try to do my best for you." He was still under the trees and, because of the pain in his knee, he

was not able to walk in a straight line yet. He stumbled slightly and wobbled a bit, bumping into the tree-trunk with his bony body. Next moment something dropped with a plopping sound onto his load followed by a small branch and some leaves from the tree above. The local man stopped and stared for a moment.

"Hello, Toad," he said with a chuckle. "What are you doing this far from home?"

Toad was speechless. First he was obviously alive, second he was on the back of another camel and still going in the wrong direction and thirdly a human had spoken to him. No "Croak, croak" from this fellow.

The snake glared down from the tree and hissed loudly, but Toad was safe, and so he shouted some abuse at the snake. "Yah, you hissy-wissy-sissy," yelled Toad. "You missed me!"

After a while, Old Camel spoke. "Are you the Toad that I saw in Churchtown last night who is going to Wellybelly?"

"That is correct," replied Toad.

"I wondered what had happened to you. You must have got into the wrong sack," said Old Camel with what sounded like a chuckle in his voice. Toad felt his temper begin to rise, but needing all the help and support he could get he stayed as calm as he could and mumbled, "Yes, I suppose I must have."

Eventually Old Camel made a throaty noise, indicating that he was getting ready to say something else, so Toad waited. "Well, you are here now but I need to explain something to you. We are going to Wangeriy first," said Old Camel, "and then we go to Bankstown."

Toad listened and felt very glum. He was still traumatized by his near-death experience and the fact that a human had spoken to him. The news from Old Camel was the last thing he needed to hear. Wangeriy and Bankstown were not where he wanted to go. He wanted to go to Wellybelly.

The ordeal with the snake had been too much for Toad. He crept into the sack for a rest and, as he drifted off, he heard the local man say to Old Camel, "Let him rest for a while". So Toad allowed himself to fall into a deep sleep.

* * *

Toad had slept for some time. Although it was still light, the shadows had lengthened indicating that it was later in the afternoon. Toad crept out of the sack, feeling refreshed and ready to find out more about his predicament. He looked around for the man who knew him so he could ask him some questions, but he was nowhere to be seen.

Toad rather reluctantly began to talk to Old Camel. "Hello, my friend, how is your leg?" Toad surprised himself that he was interested in someone else's health. Old Camel had had plenty of time to think whilst Toad was asleep, and he replied a bit more quickly than usual.

"My leg is still quite sore, so my kind keeper has tied me to this bush and has gone to look for some stronger medicine," he said.

"I think you were really brave taking that beating and then saving my life," said Toad. "If there is ever anything I can do to help, ask me and I will do everything I can."

Old Camel thought that he had not been brave at all and, as for saving Toad's life, all he had done was to limp on his bad leg, stumble about and end up by chance bumping into the tree where Toad was sitting. It was still a mystery to the camel how Toad had managed to get into the tree in the first place, never mind being able to jump onto his back at precisely the time he was passing underneath. Old Camel was hurting, and thinking when he was hurting made it difficult for him to speak, so he simply said, "Thank you, Toad."

Toad was becoming impatient. He began to look around for the local man and in the distance, coming from the direction of Churchtown, he saw movement. Walking towards them on the pathway was a human being. As the man came closer and closer, Toad could see that this man was another local, but not the one who had spoken to him earlier. He appeared about the same height, but was not as well built.

How strange, thought Toad. *Another local man!*

The man approached the old camel and looked puzzled to find him tied up and alone. Toad didn't know who this person was, so he kept quiet, and so did Old Camel.

The local man spoke. "Hi, Old Camel, you look like you've been hurt." He examined Old Camel's leg. "I suppose Jeri's gone to look for something to help you," he added and then went and sat down on a large rock, crossed his legs and settled down.

About half an hour passed and Toad was feeling very frustrated, stuck out here, still miles from Wellybelly. Toad really wanted to see the first man who had spoken to him because then he might be able to get help from him. Instead he was stuck with Old Camel, who wasn't in charge of where they were going, and another local man who Toad thought must be really stupid, just sitting there and doing nothing.

It was also getting darker as the sun began to set. Toad was thinking to himself, *Today is Thursday, tomorrow is Friday and I'm getting married on Saturday.* As he was still going in the wrong direction, it began to look less and less likely that he would manage to get back to Wellybelly by Saturday. It was an extremely worrying situation.

He was about to get really cross and start complaining to Old Camel when he saw someone walking towards them from the north. Lit up by the setting sun, the man was walking across the scrubland, weaving in and out of the bushes growing there. He appeared to be carrying a large bunch of leaves and some long plant fronds. As he came nearer and nearer, Toad could see it was Jeri, the man who had spoken to him, and suddenly he was happy again.

"Look, old Camel, look! Your kind doctor is coming to fix your leg," Toad said.

Old Camel raised his head. He said quietly, "I do hope so, for I am not sure if I can walk any further."

When Jeri arrived he began treating the camel immediately, applying the leaves with some gooey substance and holding them in place with long plant fronds which he tied around Old Camel's leg. They appeared to hold everything in place. Then Jeri turned to the other man and asked, "What brings you here?"

"Your grandfather has fallen and needs your help," the man replied. "I've come to help with the camel train so you can go back to the village."

Toad couldn't hear everything they said, but from the look on Jeri's face, it was not good news. Eventually he came over and spoke to Old camel and Toad.

"My grandfather is not well and I must go back to see him very soon," he explained. "Old Camel, you will have to stay here until the sun goes down and rest your leg. My friend will stay with you and, in the morning, you should be well enough to travel on. As for you, Toad, my friend will then take you to Wangeriy, but he does not speak to animals, so you must ask me now whatever you need to know and I will do my best to answer you before I leave."

Toad had many questions, but he restricted himself to making it clear to Jeri how important it was that he got back for his marriage celebrations. Jeri said to Toad, "There won't be any camel trains going back the other way before next Monday. The best thing is for you to stay with Old Camel. This camel train will then join another six camels in Wangeriy and then go on to Bankstown. There has been a very large thunderstorm in the Western Mountains that has washed away a bridge over the new black road and two villages close to the Southern River have been badly damaged."

Toad interrupted. "But will I be able to get to Wellybelly by Saturday?"

"The villages are cut off and are without food and fresh water. That is why the arrangements with the camel train have changed. Now, Toad, although the camel train is not going directly to Wellybelly, it will pass very nearby, and with a bit of luck, my friend here could leave the camel train and deliver you to Wellybelly before sunset on Saturday."

Before he left, Jeri explained his grandfather was called Jumbe and he was head of the village. It was Jumbe who had originally been given the gift of speaking to animals. Jeri also had the gift and Jumbe had helped him to learn how to use it when he was very young. Jumbe was a very special man in many ways and Jeri could not let him down when he needed him most.

Toad heard Jeri talking to his friend, who was called a very long name that Toad could not pronounce. It sounded like Teerumaningeri, so Toad decided that as it began with a letter T that Toad would call him Tee.

Jeri explained to Tee that it was very important to try to get Toad back to Wellybelly by Saturday, and his friend nodded. It was obvious that he held Jeri in high esteem.

Chapter Three

Friday

Jeri slipped away in the early hours of Friday morning whilst all the others were sleeping. He had a long way to go to see Jumbe, but he decided to walk through the shrubland as it was the shortest route. Although still a strong man, Jumbe had fallen and hurt himself. He was apparently unable to walk properly and the whole of his left side was very sore, but he insisted on trying to carry on as if nothing had happened. His relations were worried that he might have another fall, but they were powerless to stop him. As a last resort they had sent for Jeri, and Jumbe had agreed to rest and wait for his favourite grandson to arrive. However it would take Jeri a few hours to get to his village.

Jeri was halfway there by the time Old Camel, Toad and Tee set off for Wangeriy. Toad decided to pass the time of day with Old Camel.

"You seem to be moving better today, my friend," said Toad. "I do hope the medicine Jeri gave you will last a long time."

Toad wasn't worried now about how long the animal took to answer. He was stuck with him on the road to Wangeriy and there was no one else to talk to. Old Camel was the only friend he had in the world right now, so he was becoming more and more patient.

"Hello, Toad," said Old Camel. "The medicine appears to be working very well because I can't feel any pain in my leg, but I'm not sure how long it will last before I feel the pain again."

The road started to turn towards the west and Toad became excited. "At last," he said out loud, "we are on our way to Wellybelly!" Old Camel heard all this and didn't say anything because he didn't want to dampen Toad's enthusiasm, but he knew that Wellybelly was still a long way away. In fact Old Camel wasn't sure if Toad would make it to Wellybelly.

It was fairly early on Friday when Tee and the Old Camel

arrived in Wangeriy. Wangeriy was a larger town than either Churchtown or Bankstown and it was the gateway to the south and east of the country. There was no black road or railway linking up to Wangeriy, but there were plans for them. Within two years Wangeriy would have a black road link to the southern town of Waterford City where there was a railway connection to the east of the country.

As Billy had arrived only just a short time before them, Tee assumed he must have stopped for a rest as well. Tee went to see the boss whom he called Mr Johnson. Mr Johnson was almost bald and appeared older than he was. However he was very fit and he was taller and heavier than his son Billy and towered over Tee.

"Hi, Mr Johnson," said Tee, "Jeri's had to go back to the village to see his grandfather so I will help until he returns to the camel train."

Mr Johnson nodded to Tee and came over to look at Old Camel. "He doesn't look too well does he, Tee? What's happened?" he asked. Tee told him what Billy had done and how Jeri had helped Old Camel.

Mr Johnson checked the repairs to Old Camel's leg and nodded in appreciation of the work Jeri had done. Then he called his son over. Billy walked over to his father, looking sulky and disinterested. Mr Johnson grumbled at his son, who tried to blame Jeri and then the camel, but Mr Johnson would have none of it. He gave his son a lecture on how to behave with animals, how to take responsibility for their safety and how to look after the customers whose goods were loaded onto the camels' backs. The son said something rude to his father and Mr Johnson ended up by kicking Billy in the backside.

Mr Johnson arranged for all the goods to be unloaded as they were for customers in Wangeriy. This worried Toad. "What am I going to do?" he whispered to Old Camel. "If they take me off and leave me here I'll never get to Wellybelly."

About five minutes passed by before Old Camel spoke, letting out a big sigh as he did. "PHYEEW!" he said. Toad didn't seem to understand that interpreting Toad into camel language and then speaking to Toad in his language was easier for some camels than for others. However he was doing his best. Maybe he did make a mistake here and there, but all you can do is your best. Old Camel was becoming very weary. He said firmly, "Toad, Jeri has given Tee instructions. Please be patient. Stay hidden and I'm sure he will find you and load you back up again."

Most of the other camels were already loaded and ready to go because of the urgency of getting supplies to the flooded villages. Mr Johnson decided he was going to set off with his son and take five of their own camels. He gave instructions to Tee and another man called Mantupo to follow on with four more camels, another one from Wangeriy and the remaining three from the original camel train. He said to Tee, "If we get there earlier than you, then at least we can give the flood victims some relief. Please make sure Old Camel is fully ready before you travel and let him rest when necessary."

Tee knew that Mr Johnson had a soft spot for Old Camel because he was the first camel he had ever owned. "Yes, Boss," he said. "We'll follow on in about four hours. Mantupo and I will take care and we'll look after Old Camel. Safe journey, Mr Johnson."

Billy was really angry. He had seen the others smile as his father had rebuked him. He hated camels, he hated the men who worked with them and he hated his father. Someone was going to have to pay for his humiliation.

Tee assembled the loads for the four camels. He managed to find a small package that was lighter than the others and which fitted easily onto Old Camel's back. It also had a small opening in the corner. Tee didn't say anything, but he smiled at Toad as he squeezed him into the small opening.

"Hey, steady on Tee," cried Toad. "Be careful, that hole's a bit small for me." He was worrying that he might be too fat to go through it.

"Croak, croak" said Tee and as if he understood what Toad had said, he made the opening wider so Toad could get in and out.

The four-camel train with Toad on board was ready to set off by mid-afternoon. Toad was on his way! "Whoopee, we're off!" he said excitedly to Old Camel. "Thank you for being my friend. Thank you also for being patient and helping me to stay calm."

Old Camel didn't want to dampen Toad's spirit. He loved Toad's company when he was happy as he was so different from when they had first met. He just said, "Hold tight, Toad. We still have a long way to go and it will not be an easy journey." *At least, it won't be easy for me*, thought Old Camel, but he didn't voice his fears. Then he said, trying to sound positive, "But I'm determined to do my best."

* * *

Jeri was nearing his village. The sun was high in the sky and it beat down ferociously, but Jeri had grown up in this land, so he was used to the temperature and he continued to make good time.

He was looking forward to seeing Jumbe and hoping that he would be sensible and do as his grandson asked. Although Jeri had not received his skill at talking to animals from his mother, she had given him a good knowledge of medicine, including plants that helped to heal broken bones and leaves that helped with sprains, cuts and bruises. With his mother's guidance Jeri had extended his knowledge and he had made many trips across the land to find new and different medicines. Jumbe was a stubborn old man, and although Jeri's mother could have helped him, he was too proud to let her. That was why Jeri had to return.

Jeri was also aware that other people in the Western Mountains needed his help. Although most of them were originally from another land and didn't know the ways of the Western Mountains, they had chosen to live there and they needed help. Mr Johnson was a good man and wanted to help the people in trouble. That was good enough for Jeri.

Jeri thought about Old Camel and Toad and hoped that Billy hadn't caused any more trouble. Tee was his cousin and was also a very good friend, and he knew that Tee would do what he could to help Toad get back to Wellybelly in time.

* * *

Mr Johnson's camel train had not been going for more than a few hours when they came upon the first signs of the damage caused by the flooding. Mr Johnson's original plan had been to cross the Southern River at a shallow ford some miles south of Bankstown and then head north to the village on the far side of the river. However, when he arrived at the ford, the Southern River was in full flow and carrying debris fast downstream. It was obviously too dangerous to cross, so Mr Johnson decided to take an alternative route. He would now have to turn north earlier than planned and travel up to Bankstown where there was a substantial bridge. Provided the bridge wasn't damaged, they could cross there.

He let Billy know his plans and took the route known as 'Rocky Road'. He knew Tee was a good tracker and that he would realize what had happened and follow them.

* * *

It was late afternoon when Jeri finally arrived home. The children of the village ran to greet him when they saw him coming. He was very popular with the children and they greeted him with songs and clapped their hands and laughed.

As he entered the village, Jeri's mother and two of the elders met him. "Jumbe is a stubborn old man, Jeri," said his mother. "We are sorry to bring you all this way, but I think he has used this opportunity to see you."

"Mother, I understand," said Jeri. "Please take me to him. Give me about one hour with him, then please bring me your medicine box."

Jeri knew he could get the better of Jumbe if he just spent some time with him. They would talk and ask each other about what had happened since the last time they met and eventually Jumbe would ask him to look at his injuries. Respect for elders was important to the native people and it was necessary to go through this ritual if Jeri was to be allowed to treat his grandfather.

Jeri walked into Jumbe's lodge to find him lying down resting.

"Hello, Grandfather" he said. "It's really good to see you, but I had hoped the circumstances would be better."

Jumbe beckoned Jeri to sit down next to him and replied, "I was being really silly Jeri, trying to do something a man of your age could do."

He shook his head at the thought of his failure and then asked Jeri what he had been doing. He was not surprised to hear that he had been helping Mr Johnson to deliver relief to the villages damaged by the floods.

Jumbe had met Mr Johnson once and had been impressed by him. As a newcomer to this land, Mr Johnson had respect for people, animals, trees and plants. Jumbe heard about the damage caused by the flood and grumbled about how silly the people had been to build homes where they had. He also felt a little bit guilty that he had asked his grandson to abandon the camel train and come to see him, but nevertheless he was immensely proud of the young man. Family was really important to Jumbe and it seemed to him that family was also important to Jeri.

Finally, after about an hour, Jumbe said, "Come on, Jeri, please get me fixed up and then you can be on your way to help Mr Johnson. The people in the flooded villages need your help." He smiled. "Jeri, you really shouldn't have come all this way. I'm sure your mother could have managed without you." Jeri smiled at Jumbe but said nothing.

* * *

When the four-camel train came to a halt, Tee was at the back of the train with Old Camel. Tee walked to the front of the train and spoke to Mantupo.

"What's wrong, Mantupo?" he asked. Mantupo pointed to the tracks of the camels where Mr Johnson and his camel train had turned north. On seeing the Southern River in full flow, Tee understood immediately why Mr Johnson had changed his plans. Although Mr Johnson knew the area, he hadn't travelled this route for many years and would have forgotten just how bad the road he had taken was. Obviously he had decided to go to Bankstown this way as the river was too dangerous to cross and the only realistic chance anybody had was to use the bridge there.

It was getting dark and the setting sun in the west cast long shadows of the camel train. Tee and Mantupo decided they should rest where they were and then set off for Bankstown at first light the following morning.

"Tomorrow is Saturday," said Toad to Old Camel. "Do you think we will be able to get to Wellybelly before tomorrow night?"

Old Camel thought long and hard before answering. He had felt a few small pains in his knee during the last minutes before they had stopped. Eventually he answered Toad, "We are travelling to Bankstown, and as we are on this side of the river, we will be nearer to Wellybelly. However the road we are travelling on is known as the 'Rocky Road' with lots of uneven ground, so it will take us longer. Whether my knee will stand up to the conditions only time will tell."

Toad felt a bit down after hearing this news and said the only thing he could. "Old Camel, without you I would die out here, so please take care and rest when you need to."

Old Camel was surprised to hear Toad talking this way. On the journey together they had become good friends, because Toad had lost some of his pomposity and had become more considerate to others.

"If we manage to make it to Bankstown," continued Old Camel, "the road to Wellybelly is a lot easier and I'm sure I will be able to manage that part of the journey."

"Let's rest then," said Toad. "You are going to need all your strength by the sound of it."

"Goodnight, Toad," said Old Camel.

"Goodnight, Old Camel," said Toad. "Sleep well."

* * *

Mr Johnson's camel train was having a tough time. It was such a long time since he had travelled this way to Bankstown that he had forgotten just how bad the trail was. However he didn't have a choice as it was the only place where there was a bridge to cross the river.

They had to travel over several parts of the track, which climbed in places and had large rocks in the way. Billy was particularly unhelpful, sulking and grumbling about everyone and everything. Mr Johnson made his mind up to speak to the boy again but at this moment he needed all the help he could get.

At last, as dusk was falling on Friday evening, Mr Johnson saw the lights of Bankstown. With a bit of luck they would arrive before it became totally dark. He worried that Old Camel would not make it to Bankstown, but he trusted Tee and knew he would take great care and rest the old beast when needed.

The camel train eventually arrived at Bankstown at nightfall. They camped about one mile south of where the bridge was and decided to wait until dawn. Billy, however, had no intention of going any further with this camel train. He was fed up with his father's discipline and thought he would take this opportunity to leave once and for all. He stole some food and fresh water that had been meant for the flood victims, put it into his backpack and slipped away into the night. He decided to head for Wellybelly where he would take the black road to the west. He could hitch a lift to the coast and get some work on a boat and pay his passage back to the country where his mother lived.

Mr Johnson's wife had left him years before and gone back to their homeland with another man, leaving her husband to bring up Billy all on his own. During the journey, Billy had not paid any attention to anything his father had said, so he did not know that the black road was impassable.

Chapter Four

Saturday

Jeri treated Jumbe's injury, but told him as sternly as he could that rest was his best cure. He said there were some plants that grew in the marshy area by the side of Wellybelly Lake which would aid his recovery and remove some of the soreness. He told his grandfather he would bring some back after he had helped the people in the flooded area.

Jumbe insisted that Jeri stay the night. After a proper night's rest and some good food, he could set off early on Saturday morning and be fresh for the journey. In truth Jeri sat up most of the evening, firstly playing with the children of the village, and then sitting round with the elders discussing all things important to the villagers. For a young man he was thought to be very wise and his opinion was listened to. Jeri was really tired when he finally lay down and he slept deeply. Next morning Jeri rose at dawn, took his mother's medicine bag and some food with him and set off in the direction of Wellybelly.

* * *

Meanwhile at Bankstown, Mr Johnson went up to the bridge and surveyed the situation. Thankfully the bridge was intact. He met with some of the people from the town, told them what his plans were and listened in return to what they said. News had come through from the flooded villages. Whilst the larger village on the far side of the river could be reached by crossing the bridge, it would be easier to get to the smaller village by travelling towards Wellybelly. Then they must turn and follow the black road as far as the damaged area and they would find the other villages close by.

Several people offered to help and were prepared to travel with the camel train to help unload and assist the victims to rebuild their homes. Mr Johnson selected four of the strongest-looking men to travel with them. After further discussions,

Mr Johnson, decided to take his own camel train across the bridge and deliver aid to the larger village, leaving the smaller one to Tee's camel train. That would make life easier for Old Camel. He spoke to a man called Jim Edwards, who seemed to be important in Bankstown, and explained that a second camel train was a few hours behind. He told Jim about the limitations of Old Camel and asked him to redirect this train via Wellybelly and then up to the other village. Jim was particularly helpful and Mr Johnson felt confident that Tee would get the message. Mr Johnson was concentrating so much on the task that he completely forgot about Billy. He set off for the flooded area unaware that Billy had left.

* * *

Jeri set off in the direction of Wellybelly and was taking the quickest route to the western side of the lake. He was about halfway to Wellybelly when he reached the crossroads. One pathway went to Churchtown and the other to Wellybelly. There were two other little-used tracks; the easterly track went to the badlands and the westerly track led back towards Croco Lake. He decided to take the track to Croco Lake knowing that there was a turn that would lead him to the western side of Wellybelly Lake.

He had been travelling for about half an hour when he noticed the landscape was changing as he got nearer to Wellybelly. The land had become wetter underfoot and in particular the wooded area east of the Western Mountains appeared to be waterlogged. Jeri's curiosity got the better of him. He wandered farther off course, getting into wetter and wetter areas, ankle-deep in parts. Unknown to Jeri, Croco Lake in the east of the mountains had started to overflow with all the water from the storm. The water had spilled through the wooded area onto the plains, covering the lower parts of the bushes that grew there. Jeri was also completely unaware that some of the crocodiles that lived in Croco Lake had started to move from the lake, following the water that had spilled onto the plain. They were looking for food.

Jeri had been tramping through the wet area for some time when he noticed some splashing in the distance. Again curiosity got the better of him, so he walked steadily towards the splashing. What he saw shocked him. Crocodiles, three of them, were eating a small deer. Rather belatedly, he realized what must have happened - Croco Lake had burst its banks.

Jeri couldn't talk to crocodiles, but he knew they had been on this land from prehistoric times and had no respect for anyone or anything. They seemed to kill indiscriminately, and seeing them sent a shiver down Jeri's back. Where there were one or two crocodiles, there were bound to be more. There were many crocodiles living in the Croco Lake and Croco River area, and the worry for Jeri was that the floodwater would reach Wellybelly Lake and the crocodiles would reach Toad's home.

It was now midday on Saturday. Jeri decided to climb a tree and see if he could find out how far the floodwater had spread. He selected the tallest tree in the area and, after climbing it, he looked in the direction of Wellybelly towards a slightly raised bank. He was relieved to see that the water appeared to be a long way below the bank, because he knew that if the water could not reach Wellybelly Lake, then neither would the crocodiles.

He was about to climb down and make his way to safety when he noticed that the three crocodiles were waiting for him at the bottom of his tree. Jeri was going nowhere.

* * *

Tee's four-camel train had set off just as the sun rose. They would have a few hours before the hottest part of the day. Hopefully they would have reached Bankstown by then and got the most difficult part of the journey out of the way.

It was uncomfortable for all the camels, but in particular for Old Camel who was having a really hard time. After about an hour on the Rocky Road his knee gave way and he stumbled, unable to travel any further. He fell down on the ground and his legs splayed out. He cried out to Toad, "I can't go on! I'm sorry, but I can't go on!"

Tee saw what had happened to the old camel and shouted to Mantupo to stop. Immediately he took part of the load off Old Camel's back, tied one of the camel's leads around its body and attached the lead to Gruff Camel. With the help of Gruff Camel he managed to pull Old Camel into a standing position. Without his full load Old Camel could probably just get to Bankstown where Tee could re-evaluate the situation. So he redistributed half of Old Camel's load onto the other three camels.

They set off again and Toad tried to keep Old Camel's spirits up, speaking to him in his softest, most gentle voice. "Well done, my old friend," said Toad when he got over a particularly difficult hill and "you can do it!" when it seemed as though the poor creature couldn't take another step. There wasn't much else Toad could do except keep giving his support. Old Camel felt like giving up on three or four occasions, but with help from Tee and gentle persuasion from Toad, finally the camel train came in sight of Bankstown.

There was some really good news for Toad and Old Camel when they reached Bankstown. A man called Jim Edwards greeted the camel train and explained what Mr Johnson wanted Tee to do. Toad heard this and shouted out loud, "Yippee! We're going to Wellybelly, we're going to Wellybelly!"

Although they had rested for an hour, Old Camel's knee was beginning to swell again and Tee examined him and made a decision. He didn't think Old Camel could get to the small village, so he decided to split his train into two. He would travel with Old Camel and Gruff Camel to Wellybelly and leave Old Camel there by the Lake where there was plenty of grazing. That would give him time to recover from his injury. He would then put Old Camel's part-load onto Gruff Camel and follow on. His diversion should not take more than an hour and he would soon catch up with the others. He didn't tell Mantupo that he would also deliver Toad to Wellybelly, as he had promised Jeri he would do.

* * *

Billy had now eaten his food and drunk his water. He had underestimated just how hard it was to walk in this landscape in the dark and on your own. After hearing night-time creature noises, he became frightened, so he found a big stick made of very hard wood. That should protect him against anything.

He had set off during the night, and as the sun rose, he suddenly became very tired. He walked on until the sun became unbearably hot and found a large rock offering some shade. Feeling tired through lack of sleep, he decided to rest for a while and eventually he fell asleep.

He was awakened by the sound of voices. He peeped out from behind the large rock and saw four camels passing by with two handlers. Billy had no idea of the time, but the sun was high in the sky. After the two men had finished talking, he watched as one man took two camels in a westerly direction towards the black road and the other man took the remaining two camels in the direction of Wellybelly Lake.

When Billy recognized them, he became very angry. The man known as Tee was leading the two camels that had got him into trouble and was heading for Wellybelly. Tee was the man who had smirked when his father had disciplined him. He decided he would follow them and take his revenge by stealing all the food and drink that was on the camels' backs. After that he would work out what to do next.

He watched Tee and the two camels as they walked eastwards towards Wellybelly Lake. He followed them, keeping well out of sight. Half-an-hour later Tee and the two camels arrived at the first part of the Lake. Tee tied up Old Camel and, after getting him to sit down, he reached into the load on the camel's back and took Toad out. When Toad realized where he was, he couldn't contain himself. '"I'm going to be married, I'm going to be married!" he sang. Old Camel had never heard Toad so happy. "Toad, I am so pleased for you" he said. "I will wish you all the best with your getting married, whatever that is."

Toad shouted his thanks across to Gruff Camel and said to both of them, "Remember we are all now friends and I meant what I said – if you ever need my help, I will come. All you need to do is ask."

They said their goodbyes and the two camels felt sad that the trip had come to an end. It had been interesting and exciting, and had been nothing like the normal camel train trips. Toad had certainly been very entertaining and they were going to miss him.

Tee walked for several minutes with Toad and then left him by the edge of the lake. There were hundreds of toads all swimming about.

"Hi guys, I'm back!" shouted Toad. "Take me to the girls."

"Croak, croak," said Tee, but nobody heard him.

Tee walked back to the camels and saw a man who he recognized as Billy, leaning over Old Camel and taking things out of his load. Old Camel's load had blankets and other household items, but no food. Billy was furious and in anger, he began throwing the blankets about. "Where's the food?" he screamed. He began to prod Old Camel with the big stick just as Tee arrived.

"Hey, Billy" Stop hurting that poor camel!" yelled Tee. Billy turned round and with a roar of anger he charged at Tee, swinging the big stick at him. Tee moved quickly out of the way but caught his foot on a large stone and fell over, twisting his ankle badly. He cried out in pain and grasped hold of his ankle. On seeing Tee lying defenceless, Billy gloated. "I'll come back and sort you out later," he said. Billy was really wild. He was also very hungry and thirsty. He went over to Old Camel again and started to re-check the load. Finding no food or water he began prodding Old Camel's bad leg again with the stick and shouted out loudly to Tee. "Where is the food?" Old Camel screamed out, but Billy wasn't concerned. Tee shouted back Billy. "The food isn't here. All we have is blankets and clothing." Billy screamed out again only louder. Old Camel was sitting on the floor and was crying. He looked really frightened.

Seeing all this, Gruff Camel knew he had to do something, otherwise if Billy continued to hurt Old Camel his friend would never walk again. He hurried over to Billy and came up behind him. Billy didn't hear Gruff Camel because of Old Camel's crying, but suddenly felt a searing pain in his arm as Gruff Camel bit him. Billy had never known a pain like it, and screamed loudly. He was frightened the camel would bite him

again, so he ran off in the direction of Churchtown where he crossed the black road and disappeared into some scrubland.

Gruff Camel felt very guilty. Billy was Mr Johnson's son and he liked Mr Johnson. What would he say when he found out? Gruff Camel waited and waited. He was very upset that Old Camel was so badly injured, and as Tee was hurt as well, there was nobody to help him.

Or was there?

It was getting late, and Gruff Camel knew what he had to do. He had to find Toad. He would know what to do. It was becoming too dark to find him now, so he decided to wait until Sunday morning.

* * *

Late on Saturday Mr Johnson had arrived at the larger village by the Southern River and seen the desperate plight of the people there. They were so pleased that someone had managed to bring help that they cheered and clapped with relief.

Things were worse than Mr Johnson had thought. Homes had been completely washed away and it was obvious to anyone who saw the path the river took from the mountains that some of the homes should not have been built where they had. However the community spirit was strong and those people who had built on higher ground out of the path of the floodwater had taken in the homeless. The food, water and blankets brought by the camel train were very useful and the people were grateful, but they would need more than emergency supplies to rebuild their homes and their lives.

Mr Johnson agreed that on his return he would send a telegraph to the State Authorities and would try to ensure that help was given to the people who wished to rebuild their homes. He also said that he would ask the State Authorities to repair the damaged black road. He travelled farther up the side of the Southern River and looked across the raging torrent to the other, smaller village. The same thing appeared to have happened there with homes being washed away. However, in the distance he could only see two camels approaching and he was worried about what had happened to the other two. But as Mr Johnson and his men were very tired, they decided to rest there Saturday night and then set off back to Bankstown at first light on Sunday morning.

* * *

Billy was really hurting. He ran a short way into the scrubland and hid in some bushes, where he decided to examine his arm. The pain in his arm had not subsided, and as he saw where Gruff Camel had bitten him, he realised that his skin was beginning to turn purple. It looked as though the camel might have bitten down to the bone. Billy was worried that the wound would become infected and a sickly feeling rose in his throat.

Sitting down with his back against a rock, he wondered how his life had become so bad. He had missed his mother when she left home and his father didn't seem to understand him. Billy knew times were changing and he had asked his father about getting a new form of transport. What they needed was a truck that could deliver parcels up and down the black road. Billy felt his father was still stuck in the old ways, unaware of the changes that were taking place. Billy didn't really hate camels - they just stood in the way of progress. Camels would be needed for lots of the journeys where black roads would never go, but trucks had to be the future.

He felt very sorry for himself, and eventually became quite dizzy and slipped into unconsciousness.

Chapter Five

Sunday

Toad had a wonderful evening. In fact it lasted from late on Saturday to the early hours of Sunday morning. There were so many lady toads for him to cuddle that he wondered why he had ever worried about not finding a wife. He was very contented, and after he had snuggled up to his chosen wife, who was big and cuddly, he fell into a very deep sleep.

Early on Sunday morning, whilst Toad was in the middle of a beautiful dream, he was woken up suddenly by a terrible roar. All of the toads in Wellybelly Lake had shouted "CAMEL!" at the same time. What was going on?

* * *

Meanwhile, Jeri had had to spend Saturday night in the tree. He had lodged himself between two big branches and hoped he wouldn't fall out of the tree in the night. He also hoped that the crocodiles would have gone, but as dawn broke on Sunday morning, he was dismayed to see that under his tree there were now seven of them.

Jeri was not to know, but these were the only crocodiles that had left Croco Lake. The water seemed to have ceased to flow from the lake, but the area was still quite boggy. He wondered about escaping, but knew he needed help. Looking around, he scanned the horizon for any birds. If he could find a bird, perhaps he could send a message to Jumbe asking for help. He kept looking, but there were no birds within range for as far as he could see.

* * *

As dawn broke on Sunday morning, Gruff Camel saw that Tee had dragged himself across the ground and was lying next to Old Camel. Billy was nowhere to be seen.

46

The next thing that needed to happen would be the biggest challenge in Gruff Camel's life. He thought to himself, *How am I going to find Toad in a lake full of toads?*

Gruff Camel knew that Tee had walked quite a way with Toad when he had taken him to his 'wedding', whatever that was, so he wandered to the far end of the Lake. When he arrived there, he took a deep breath and shouted as loudly as he could, "TOAD!"

Within an instant, hundreds of toads shouted back, "CAMEL!"

Oh dear, thought Gruff Camel, *what do I do now?* After a few minutes, when he had thought of something else to say, he shouted loudly again, "I WANT TO SPEAK TO THE TOAD WHO IS MY FRIEND." There were no replies.

Gruff Camel suddenly began to feel sad. He wondered if Toad had forgotten him, or maybe he was in another part of the Lake and unable to hear him. Time continued to pass before a worried Gruff Camel galvanized himself to shout the same message again even more loudly than before. If this didn't work, he would have to try shouting for Toad in another part of the Lake. Would Toad ever hear him? "I WANT TO SPEAK TO THE TOAD WHO IS MY FRIEND," bellowed Gruff Camel again.

Gruff Camel was looking out over the Lake when he heard a familiar voice coming from the water's edge. "Hey, Gruff Camel, I'm not deaf, you know. What can I do to help?"

Toad had heard the roar when Gruff Camel had first spoken. He stopped cuddling his new wife, and when he heard Gruff Camel call the second time, he started to travel to the shore, pushing his way past all the other toads. He had just arrived when Gruff Camel bellowed the third time.

"Oh dear, Toad, there's a lot of trouble." said Gruff Camel. "Billy has attacked Tee, he has hurt Old Camel and I have bitten Billy."

"When did this happen?" asked Toad.

"Just as it grew dark," said Gruff Camel. "I have worried all night long."

"OK," said Toad. "I'm here now and I am going to help you. Kneel down, put your head on the floor and I will try to climb on."

Because of the load that was still on his back, Gruff Camel struggled to do as Toad had asked, but eventually he managed it.

"Take care I don't fall off," warned Toad. "I need time to think."

Gruff Camel did as Toad asked and walked slowly back to the scene of the attack. Toad needed to assess the situation, to see how bad everything was. When they arrived back to where Old Camel and Tee were, it was obvious that Old Camel was exhausted and needed help urgently. Tee was weary and tired and looked like he was unable to stand up. Billy was nowhere to be seen.

Toad spoke to Old Camel. "We need Jeri's help, old friend," he said.

A while went by before Old Camel replied, "Jeri's a long way away in his village. How can we get him here?"

"We need to find a bird who can take a message to him," said Toad. "They can get to Jeri quicker than anyone."

"You are clever, "said Old Camel eventually. "I would have never thought of doing that!"

Toad stared up into the blue sky, and after a while, he said to Old Camel, "There's a bird up there high above us. Let's shout as loud as we can to get his attention".

Toad and Old Camel together shouted and shouted, "BIRD! BIRD! BIRD!" The bird eventually came down and flew backwards and forwards above them.

"Bird," begged Toad, "please can you help us?"

"What do you want, Fwog?" asked the bird.

"I am a toad," said Toad rather pompously, "not a frog".

"And I am not just a bird," said the bird with even more pomposity.

"If you are not just a bird, what are you then?" said Toad.

Old Camel had been listening to the conversation between Toad and the bird and he could see that there would be a big argument if it was allowed to carry on. He made a throaty noise, indicating to Toad that he wished to speak. Toad understood that Old Camel wanted to say something, so he waited patiently. Finally Old Camel said, "Sorry, Toad, but this is not the time to be pompous. Please ask the bird what type of bird he is."

Toad was unaware that birds had types. He thought all birds were birds, but nevertheless he took Old Camel's advice and said to the bird, "I'm sorry, Bird, but what type of bird are you?"

The bird was still being pompous and replied, "I am a hawk, of course! Everybody knows that's the most important bird of all, except Fwogtoad it seems."

Toad bit his tongue, reluctantly apologized again and said, "Sorry, Hawk, we are looking for Jeri who speaks to all the animals. My friend Old Camel is badly injured and Jeri's friend Tee is also badly hurt, so we need Jeri's help as soon as possible. Jeri was at his village, but I think he may have left now. We need his help, and quickly. Please can you find him, tell him what has happened and ask him to come as quickly as he can?"

"OK," agreed Hawk. "Mighty Hawk can help Fwogtoad." He flew away.

Five minutes later he returned. "Me can't remember lots of words" he said. "By time I find Jeri I forget."

Toad was still feeling quite upset by some of the things Hawk had said, but he was very polite and spoke as slowly and clearly as he could and gave Hawk a shortened message to take to Jeri. After about five minutes, Gruff Camel said, "I knew I could count on you Toad. You are wonderful. You said that if we were ever in trouble you would come and help and you have. What a wonderful friend you are."

I'll believe it when I see Jeri, thought Toad, but he said to Gruff Camel, "That's what friends are for. Now let's hope that Mighty Hawk understood that message."

* * *

Jeri still wasn't going anywhere. He was generally a calm and confident young man, but being stuck up a tree surrounded by crocodiles was making him agitated. He had been in the tree for a long time and the crocodiles showed no sign of moving away. They couldn't climb trees, but there were too many to try to get past and make a run for it.

Suddenly Jeri heard a voice. "Hi, Jeri! I'm Mighty Hawk and I have message for you."

Jeri looked about and eventually spotted Hawk flying backwards and forwards overhead. "What is the message?" called Jeri.

"BILLYHITTEEBILLYHITCAMELBITBILLY!" screeched Hawk. Jeri managed to understand some of this, but the bird's screeching and flying about made it hard to decipher.

"Hawk, please can you say it again but slower this time?" said Jeri.

"I try" said Hawk, and repeated the message in the same maniacal screeching voice.

"BILLYHITTEEBILLYHITCAMELBITBILLY!"

Jeri still did not fully understand the message, but he asked Hawk who the message had come from.

"FWOG!" shouted the Hawk.

"Do you mean Toad?" asked Jeri.

"Yes, FWOGTOAD" – very pompous FWOGTOAD," screeched Hawk.

Jeri ignored the insult to Toad and said to Hawk, "Hawk, can you help me to get away from these crocodiles so I can go and help Toad and Camel?"

"Easy peasy," said Hawk. "You get ready climb down tree, then run." Then he said, "I be back with friends," and something else that sounded to Jeri like "we poo poo."

Jeri waited and waited. About fifteen minutes later, he saw a large, dark shape in the sky. At first he wondered what it was, but as it grew nearer he saw that it was hundreds and hundreds of birds of all types, shapes and sizes. Without warning they swooped down to the bottom of the tree and one by one began to poo-poo on the crocodiles, screeching all the time. 'SCHPOOP, SPHLATT, SHPLODJ, THRUMPFF!' The noise was deafening as the birds dropped their loads onto the crocodiles.

Hawk shouted to Jeri above the noise. "Ha, ha! Crocodiles no like being poo-pooed on. They go soon, Jeri. Be ready climb down tree and RUUNNN! I show you way to safety."

Slowly but surely the crocodiles began to move away and the birds made sure they went, harassing them as they retreated. The birds' attack showed no sign of diminishing and Hawk saw an opportunity for Jeri to escape. He shouted, "Now, Jeri! Climb down tree and run."

Jeri did as he was told and followed Hawk out of the wetlands to safety. When he arrived at the bank, he felt exhausted. As Hawk came over to him Jeri said, "Thank you, Hawk. Without you I could have been stuck up that tree for a very long time."

"I know," said Hawk, "I am Mighty Hawk, but have no time for thank you or sit down and rest. You need go Wellybelly and help friends before they DIIIIEEE!" He screeched the word 'die' with a worrying finality.

Until now Jeri had had no idea how urgent his friends' needs were. He checked his bag, took a drink of the precious water he had brought with him, waved goodbye to Hawk and set off towards Wellybelly at a good pace. The crocodiles were a real mess and looked a sorry sight as they slithered back towards Croco Lake.

* * *

It was about midday on Sunday when Jeri arrived at Wellybelly. Toad and the camels were overjoyed to see him.

"Did Hawk find you?" asked Toad.

"Yes," said Jeri. "I was in trouble, but Hawk rescued me. However, it's a long story and I'll tell you later." He opened his medicine bag and walked over to Old Camel and Tee. Tee had not broken his ankle, but it was badly sprained and had swollen up. Jeri treated the ankle as best he could and gave him a precious drink of water.

"Thank you, Tee, for helping Toad to get to Wellybelly" he said. "If you hadn't helped him I wouldn't have been able to get here. Your ankle will take some time to recover, but I'll make you a crutch and we will have you up, hopping about." Tee smiled weakly and gave his thanks to Jeri.

Then Jeri turned his attention to Old Camel whose knee was also very swollen. Knowing that he would probably have to treat this leg again, he had brought a strong ointment mixture from his mother and set about treating the injury.

"I think I am dying, Jeri," whispered Old Camel. "Billy really hurt me and it came at the end of the long journey. I feel really poorly."

Jeri spoke reassuringly to the old animal. "It will take time and the pain will gradually get less, but it's going to be a while before we can get you to stand," he said. He was worried about Old Camel, but he had an idea. He went over to Toad and Gruff Camel and told them just how bad Old Camel was.

"We need someone to keep his spirits up and make him think of good things, not bad things," Jeri said. "I know just the person to do that."

"Who's that?" asked Toad, thinking something exciting was about to happen.

"You, Toad," said Jeri. "Please try to keep him happy for the next few hours."

Jeri carried Toad over to Old Camel and immediately Toad started to tell Old Camel about all the good things that had happened to him since they had first met. He told him that because he had Old Camel as a friend, he was now a better toad than he used to be. Toad's kind words brought a smile to Old Camel's face, but it did not last. So Toad asked, "Would you like me to sing a song to you, my dear friend?"

Old Camel didn't know what 'sing' or 'song' meant, so he just nodded to Toad in agreement.

Then Old Camel heard a noise. It came from Toad who was sitting on a small rock, lifting his foot up and down and making a strange sound. Toad suddenly started to speak, but it was different from when he spoke normally. The words that came out were:

MY NAME IS TOAD AND I'M FROM WELLYBELLY,

I'VE LIVED IN A LAKE WHICH IN PLACES CAN BE SMELLY.

I LIKE TO EAT SLUGS AND I LIKE TO EAT FLIES,

THAT'S THE TRUTH, I'M TELLING NO LIES!

I'M AN AMPHIBIAN, I'M NOT A MAMMAL

AND MY BEST FRIEND IS THE LOVELY OLD CAMEL.

Toad continued to puff his cheeks out and make spluttering noises whilst all the time moving his foot up and down on the rock. Old Camel apparently liked what he heard and lifted the left side of his face so part of his lips curled upwards. After a while he laughed his gravelly laugh, "GROOOPTH!" And again, "GROOOPTH!"

The noise Old Camel made when he laughed was more like a grating hoot, but Toad knew his friend had enjoyed his song. Then Old Camel spoke. "That was wonderful, Toad! What was it called?"

"It's a song, which I call a tap, because I tap my leg up and down," said Toad.

Old Camel misheard him. "Did you say rap, Toad?"

Toad couldn't be bothered trying to explain new words to Old Camel and just agreed with him. "Yes," he said. "It's called rap."

"I liked that Toad," said Old Camel. "You are so clever."

"Yes, my friend, I know I'm clever and you know I'm clever, but let's just keep it between ourselves, eh? Otherwise people will think I'm pompous," said Toad with a big grin on his face.

Old Camel's face changed into what could only be described as a half-smile, half-grimace and again he laughed out loud, "GROOOPTH!" Toad began to giggle as well, but he was laughing at the noise Old Camel made. It was so infectious. Jeri had heard a lot of what was going on, and he couldn't help but wonder how this friendship had managed to develop. Such an unlikely pair, but they were definitely now the best of friends and Toad had certainly improved the disposition of Old Camel.

* * *

Mr Johnson's camel train began their return journey early on Sunday morning and they reached Bankstown by midday. Mr Johnson had to make some decisions. He was concerned about the other two camels and worried that something had happened to them. He was also very worried about what had happened to his son Billy. So he asked Jim Edwards to keep an eye on his own camels while he travelled up to Wellybelly to see if he could find out what had happened to the other two camels. He knew that there was a telegraph office in

Churchtown and he would go there to send his message to the State Authorities.

* * *

Jeri checked to see if Tee was still OK and then he went over to Gruff Camel. "Where did you bite Billy?" he asked. After a few minutes, Gruff Camel related the story. He ended up feeling very sad about what had happened. He told Jeri which way Billy had run. Jeri decided it would be a good idea to take Gruff Camel and Toad with him to look for Billy. After all, if Gruff Camel had bitten Billy as badly as Jeri thought, then the animal could be needed to carry him back and Toad could be very helpful looking out for signs of Billy. So they set off, leaving Old Camel and Tee with some food to eat and a safe place to shelter.

They had travelled for some distance when Toad said to Jeri, "Why are we bothering to look for Billy after what he has done?"

"Toad," replied Jeri, "he may die if he is not treated and it is my duty to help him whether I like him or not."

"Toad," Gruff Camel butted in rather belatedly, "I only bit him to stop him hurting Old Camel. I don't want him to die."

Toad was in the process of apologizing to his friends when he spotted Billy in some bushes slumped against a rock. He shouted to Jeri, "There he is! There's Billy!" Jeri rushed over, opened his medicine bag and started to treat Billy, whose arm had become infected and was quite poorly. Jeri managed to revive him by placing some strong-smelling herbs under his nose. Then Jeri checked the camel bite that had turned his skin a reddish purple colour and began cleaning it with some liquid from his mother's medicine bag. It was obvious to Jeri that Billy needed something stronger than he had in his medicine bag and that they had to get him back to a town quickly. Jeri knew that modern doctors had medicines that were stronger and worked in different ways from Jeri's, and he also knew that this could be Billy's last chance.

* * *

Mr Johnson arrived at Wellybelly just as Jeri was about to load Billy onto Gruff Camel's back. He raced over and asked what was going on. It took him a few minutes to take in all that had happened and he was really angry that Billy had behaved so cruelly. He knew it had been hard for Billy to be raised without a mother and thought that was the reason that Billy had turned out the way he had. He felt guilty that he hadn't done enough to stop Billy from treating the camels badly, and that he should he been a better father. He said as much to Jeri.

Jeri replied, "All children have two parents for a reason. You have managed to bring up Billy on your own whilst running a business caring for camels and the camel drivers, and that cannot have been easy. But never mind about this now. It's more important to get Billy to the doctor in Churchtown as quickly as we can."

They made good progress to Churchtown, but when they reached Dr Williams' surgery it was clear that Billy was becoming worse. Dr Williams sent for his nurse, saying it was an emergency, and as soon as she arrived she began sedating Billy ready for the doctor to operate. While the operation was in progress, Mr Johnson went to the telegraph office and sent a message to the State Authorities to tell them how serious the flooding had been and what destruction it had caused. He asked for immediate help for the flooded villages with rebuilding and told them of the damage done to the black road bridge.

When Billy woke up after his anaesthetic, he found that sitting in the room with him were some familiar faces. He saw Jeri, his father and some people in white coats. Through the window he saw Gruff Camel with a toad sitting on his head. When he realized he was not dreaming, he asked, "Where am I?"

Mr Johnson explained what had happened to Billy after he had been found and apologized to his son for not being a better father. He promised Billy that he would modernize the transportation business, and whilst he carried on with the camel driving into the outlying districts, he would buy a new van for use on the black roads. He told Billy he would be able to build up a modern transport business for the future. Billy felt very guilty. He apologized for having been a bad person and promised he would try very hard to change his ways. He apologized to all the people and even asked about the old camel.

"Old Camel is on the road to recovery," said Jeri. Some of the people in the room had tears in their eyes. Toad said to Gruff Camel, "Too much sentimentality for me. Let's go back and see how Old Camel is doing, shall we?"

"Croak, croak," said everyone except Gruff Camel and Jeri who knew of course what Toad had said. Without Toad and his ability to talk to all the animals, Jeri knew that the outcome could have been so much worse. Toad was in fact a true hero.

Before Jeri left, Dr Williams spoke to him. "Jeri," he said, "you found Billy when he was very sick and, although you had treated him well, you still had the sense to bring him to me for further treatment. Your quick actions probably saved Billy's life. I would like to see you again and perhaps you can tell me about some of your herbal medicines which helped Billy survive until you brought him to me."

"Thank you, doctor," said Jeri, feeling very humble. "I only did as my mother had taught me."

Dr Williams spoke again. "Jeri, what you did was vitally important in saving Billy's life. You seem to have a natural talent for medicine. Would you like to come and see me again and perhaps we can talk about your future and see if we can help improve your knowledge?"

Jeri felt slightly embarrassed, but he said that he would call and see the doctor again. He also told the doctor what had happened to Tee and Dr Williams provided Jeri with a crutch and asked him to bring Tee back for some treatment.

Later that evening, after Jeri, Gruff Camel and Toad had arrived back at Wellybelly, Toad asked Jeri what had happened when Hawk had found him. Jeri related the story of the crocodiles and how Hawk and his friends had rescued him. On hearing Jeri's story, Old Camel began his peculiar laughing. "GROOOPTH, GROOOPTH!" he hooted. Listening to Old Camel's infectious, gravelly laugh always made Toad giggle. They were still chuckling together when Jeri and Tee left them.

Chapter Six

A Lifelong Friendship

Two weeks had passed, and in the Wellybelly area, life had gradually returned to normal. Mr Johnson had arranged for the undelivered parcels to be sent to the smaller village. He also said that Old Camel could recuperate in Wellybelly and in future he would only have light duties. Gruff Camel stayed for several days until Tee had recovered sufficiently to walk properly again and soon only Toad and Old Camel were left at the lake.

Something had been bothering Toad ever since he had started on his journey. He was still wondering how it was he had decided to climb into the sacks in the first place. However, the more he thought about it, the more confused he got. Toad and Old Camel had become great friends, and since Old Camel could now walk properly, they had met every morning and would spend the day together.

"Tell me," said Toad, "we have become the best of friends. Well, I think you are now MY best friend, anyway, but I just can't understand how it all happened. I know I had been knocked unconscious and was a bit tired for a while, but for the life of me I can't work out why I decided to climb in the sack and travel the wrong way to my wedding."

Toad had forgotten the conversation they had had the first time he had met Old Camel and how his adventure had started. Old Camel knew Toad had asked him some questions and that he had just guessed the answers. His lip curled and he began to smile. He was about to start laughing, but thought better of it.

Old Camel was well on his way to a full recovery and with his best friend Toad on his back he walked up and down by the edge of the lake. The local people had heard all about the camels who had delivered aid to the flooded villages and they were proud of them. As a result, Wellybelly now had some celebrities. Three young children from a nearby farm, a boy and his two older sisters, were regular visitors, and they were watching as Old Camel wandered into the Lake at Wellybelly and started to drink. The children were very interested in the old animal and the fat toad on his back, enjoying spending time with the heroes of Wellybelly. Old Camel always liked to drink a lot of water before going on any journey and he knew that soon he would be back at work, although it would only be light duties.

Toad watched as the young children stopped to watch Old Camel drinking.

"There's that thirsty camel again," said one little girl to the other.

The boy looked from one sister to the other, but didn't say anything.

"He's always thirsty," said the other girl.

Old Camel heard what the children said. He turned and looked at Toad. His left lip began to curl, he winked and he said "I told you I always go to Wellybelly Thursty." Old Camel couldn't contain himself, and he started to laugh again, "GROOOPTH!" and again, "GROOOPTH!"

Meanwhile, Toad couldn't believe his ears. Old Camel had said the funniest thing he'd heard in years. Toad threw back his head and laughed and laughed until the tears ran out of his eyes and splashed on the ground like puddles.

Eventually, when he got his breath back, he composed himself and found his voice. "I just love you, old friend," he said. "Without you I would have missed one of the best adventures of my life."

Eventually Old Camel replied, "Me too, Toad. Me too!"

* * *

Old Camel had found a new home grazing and drinking beside Wellybelly Lake. He knew that Mr Johnson only needed him for light duties and gradually his leg became free of pain once the swelling reduced. He couldn't remember the last time he had felt so well. Toad had stayed during the day and then went to the lake just before it went dark and they had enjoyed each other's company relating over and over again all the details of their adventure. The last time Old Camel saw Toad he had brought his wife to the edge of Wellybelly Lake. She sat with Toad on the top of some large oval stones by the water's edge, watching the sunset. Old Camel smiled at the sight of them. He knew, when it was time to leave, he would miss his friend very badly – but he was really pleased that Toad had found a wife. They looked very happy together and that was what Toad had always wanted, right from the moment they first met which now seemed a long time ago.

As darkness fell and Toad waved goodbye, slipping under the lapping water with his wife, Old Camel wondered if he would ever see his special friend again.

Join Toad, Camel and friends in their next adventure,
'TOAD and the MIRACLE AT CROCO LAKE'.

As a result of the violent storms in the Western Mountains,
disaster has befallen Croco Lake. Travelling with Jeri and
other villagers to examine what has happened at the lake,
Toad and Old Camel again run into danger and find their
lives hang in the balance once again.